· ABROAD ·

· BON VOYAGE ·

Last year, dear friends, we met "At Home,"
And now "Abroad" we mean to roam:
With all who choose to spare the time
We'll wander to a neighbouring clime.
Nor need you leave your own fireside,
For with fair Fancy for our guide,
Our wingèd thoughts, in swallow-flight,
Shall cross the Channel smooth and bright;
And in despite of wind or weather,
We'll make our little tour together.

Now on our Pictures you shall look:—
To you we dedicate our Book.

ABROAD

THOS · CRANE

ELLEN · E · HOUGHTON

Bracken Books
LONDON

First published 1882
by Marcus Ward & Co.

This edition published 1985 by Bracken Books
a division of Bestseller Publications Limited,
Brent House, 24 Friern Park, North Finchley,
London N12 9DA

and copyright © Bracken Books 1985.
ISBN 0 946495 37 8

Printed and bound by Offizin Andersen Nexö, Leipzig
German Democratic Republic.

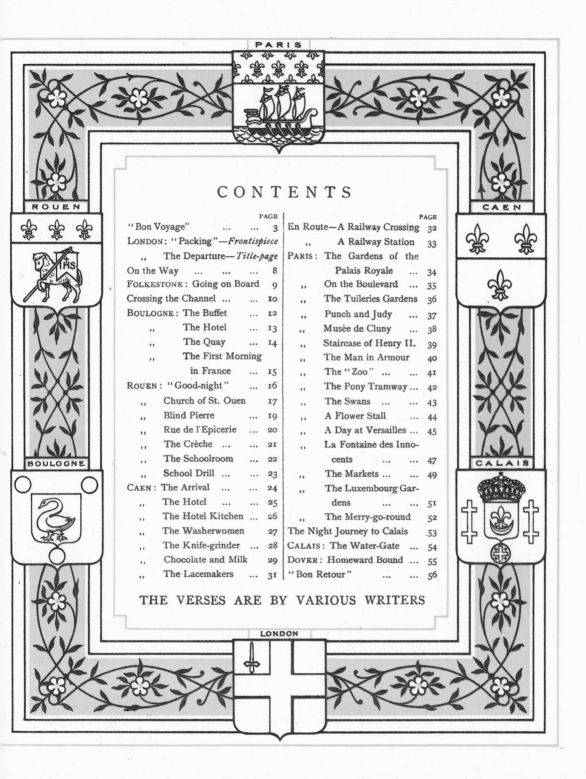

CONTENTS

THE VERSES ARE BY VARIOUS WRITERS

M Y READERS, would you like to go *abroad*, for just an hour or so,
  With little friends of different ages? Look at them in these pictured pages—
Brothers and sisters you can see,—all children of one family.
Their father, too, you here will find, and good Miss Earle, their teacher kind.
Three years ago their Mother died, and ever since has Father tried
To give his children in the Spring some tour, or treat, or pleasant thing.
Said he, last Easter, "I propose, for Nellie, Dennis, Mabel, Rose,
A trip abroad—to go with me to Paris and through Normandy."
Then all exclaimed, "Oh! glorious!"—"But may not Bertie go with us?—"
Said Rose—"We can't leave *him* at home." Then Father said he too should come.
Turn to the Frontispiece and see the children packing busily.
The next page shows them in the station at Charing Cross. Their great elation
Is written plainly on their faces.—Bell rings—"Time's up—Come, take your places!"

*　　*　　*　　*　　*

The "Folkestone Express" sped on like a dream,
And there lay the steamer fast getting up steam.

THEN at the Folkestone harbour, down they go
  Across the gangway to the boat below;
Mabel and Rose just crossing you can see,
Each holding her new doll most carefully.

Nellie, Miss Earle, and Bertie too appear,
Whilst Dennis, with the rugs, brings up the rear.
May looks behind her with an anxious air,
Lest Father, at the last, should not be there.

Our children once on board, all safe and sound,
Watch with delight the busy scene around.
The noisy steam-pipe blows and blows away,—
"Now this is just the noise we like," they say.

But while the turmoil loud and louder grows,
"I'm glad the wind blows gently," whispers Rose.
And as the steamer swiftly leaves the quay,
Mabel and Dennis almost dance with glee.

CROSSING THE CHANNEL.

THE sea is calm, and clear the sky—only a few clouds scudding by:
The Passengers look bright, and say, "Are we not lucky in the day!"
The Mate stands in the wheelhouse there, and turns the wheel with watchful care:
Steering to-day is work enough; what must it be when weather's rough?
Look at him in his sheltered place—*he* hasn't got a merry face—
'Tis not such fun for *him*, you know, he goes so often to and fro.
Nellie and Father, looking back, glance at the vessel's lengthening track—
"How far," says Nellie, "we have come! good-bye, good-bye, dear English home!"
Dennis and Rose and Mabel, walking upon the deck, are gaily talking—
Says Mabel, "No one must forget to call my new doll 'Antoinette';
Travelling in France, 'twould be a shame for her to have an English name."
Says Dennis, "Call her what you will, so you be English 'Mabel' still.
Says Rose, to Dennis drawing nigher, "I think the wind is getting higher;"
"If a gale blows, do you suppose, we shall be wrecked?" asks little Rose."

WHILE chatting with Dennis, Rose lost all her fear;
    And the swift Albert Victor came safe to the pier
At Boulogne, where they landed, and there was the train
In waiting to take up the travellers again.
But to travel so quickly was not their intent:
On a little refreshment our party was bent.
Here they are at the Buffet—for dinner they wait—
And the tall *garçon*, André, attends them in state.

At a separate table sits Monsieur Legros,
And behind him his poodle, Fidèle, you must know,
Who can dance, he's so clever, and stand on his head,
Or upon his nose balance a morsel of bread.
Mabel takes up some sugar to coax him, whilst Nell
Calls him to her—Fidèle understands very well—
"Why! he must have learnt English, he knows what we say,"
Mabel cries, "See!—he begs in the cleverest way."

THEN to the Hotel on the quay they all went;
To remain till the morrow they all were content:
After so much fatigue Father thought it was best,
For the children were weary and needed the rest.
Pictured here is the room in that very Hotel,
Where so cosily rested Rose, Mabel, and Nell.

Mabel dreamed of the morrow—of buying French toys:
Rose remembered the steam-pipe, and dreamed of its noise.
Nellie's dreams were of home, but she woke from her trance
Full of joy, just to think they were *really* in France.
     Very early next morning, you see them all three
     Looking out from their window that faces the sea.

THE FIRST MORNING IN FRANCE.

HERE they see a pretty sight,
Sunny sky and landscape bright :
Fishing-boats move up and down,
With their sails all red and brown.

Some to land are drawing near,
O'er the water still and clear,
Full of fish as they can be,
Caught last night in open sea.

On the pavement down below,
Fishwives hurry to and fro,
Calling out their fish to sell—
"What a noisy lot," says Nell,

"What a clap—clap—clap—they make
With their shoes each step they take.
Wooden· shoes, I do declare,
And oh ! what funny caps they wear!"

After breakfast all went out
To view the streets, and walk about
The ancient city-walls, so strong,
Where waved the English flag for long.

Toy shops too they went to see,
Spread with toys so temptingly :
Dolls of every kind were there,
With eyes that shut and real hair—

And, in a brightly-coloured row,
Doll-fisherfolk like these below.
Prices marked, as if to say,
"Come and buy us, quick, to-day !"

One for Mabel, one for Rose,
Two for Bertie I suppose,
Father bought.—Then all once more
Set off travelling as before.

TO Rouen next they went, that **very** day,
    And heard strange places called out by the way,
Where bells kept tinkling while the train delayed :
At Amiens ten minutes quite they stayed.

Dennis bought chocolate to make a feast—
They had *three* dinners in the train, at least.
At Rouen here they are at last, though late—
The bedroom clock there shows 'tis after eight !

Mabel looks tired—she lies back in her chair
Beside the wood fire burning brightly there.
Rose says—" Good-night !"—to Bertie fast asleep,
While her own eyes can scarcely open keep.

Next morning, through the quaint old streets of Rouen
They went to see the old church of Saint Ouen,
With eager feet, and chatting as they walked,
About the ancient Town, together talked.

SAID Dennis, first,
  "This city bold
Belonged to us
  In days of old."
Said Nellie, "Here
  Prince Arthur wept—
By cruel John
  A prisoner kept.
Here Joan of Arc
  Was tried and burned,
When fickle fate
  Against her turned."
Said Rose, "Oh dear!
  It makes me sad
To think what trouble
  People had
Who lived once in
  This very town,
Where we walk gaily
  Up and down."

17

NOW they have come into the entrance wide
  Of great St. Ouen's Church ; see, side by side,
Dennis and Nellie going on before:
The others watch yon beggar at the door—
Poor blind Pierre ; he always waits just so,
Listening for those who come and those who go.
He tells his beads, and hopes all day that some
May think of him, 'mongst those who chance to come.
Though he can't see, he is so quick to hear,
He knows a long, long time ere one draws near,
And shakes the coppers in his well-worn tin—
"Click, click," it goes—see, Bertie's gift drops in.
'Tis his *one* sou that Bertie gives away—
It might have bought him sweets this very day.
When through St. Ouen's Church they'd been at last,
Along its aisles and down its transept passed,
They went to the Cathedral, there to see
The tomb of Rolf, first Duke of Normandy.
But Mabel said, "Why should we *English* care
About that Rolf they say was buried there?"
Then she ran on, not waiting for reply—
My little reader, can *you* tell her why?

ROUEN

RUE DE L'ÉPICERIE

THE Cathedral was cold,
  With its dim solemn aisles.
But outside our friends found
The sun waiting, with smiles,
To show them their way,
So hither they came
Along an old street
With a hard French name,

And still walking onward,
Through streets we can't see,
At length reached the Crèche
Of "Sœur Rosalie"—
Where poor women's children
Are kept all day through,
Amused, taught, and tended,
And all for one *sou*.

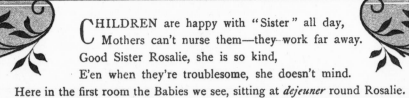

CHILDREN are happy with "Sister" all day,
  Mothers can't nurse them—they work far away.
Good Sister Rosalie, she is so kind,
  E'en when they're troublesome, she doesn't mind.
Here in the first room the Babies we see, sitting at *dejeuner* round Rosalie.

Dodo is crying, he can't find his spoon—some one will find it and comfort him soon.
  Over yon cradle bends kind Sister Claire,
  Dear little Mimi is waking up there.
  Sister Félicité, sweetly sings she,
  "Up again, down again, *Bébé*, to me."

THE school-room of the *Créche* is wide,
The children sit there, side by side,
While "Sister" hears their lessons through,
And when there's no more work to do
They all get up, and form a ring,
And as they stand, together sing.
Now hand in hand, tramp, tramp they go,
Now in a line march to and fro,
For with the rattle in her hand
The "Sister" makes them understand
When to advance and when draw back—
Click-clack it goes, click-clack, click-clack.
On Stéphanie now turn your eyes,
She's only five, but she's so wise—
She knows the alphabet all through,
And, more than that, can teach it too.
Just now, she moves her wand to J,
And tells the children what to say.
But 'tis no use to tell Ninette,
For she is but a *bébé* yet.

FRANCE

23

ARRIVAL AT CAEN.

THROUGH Rouen when our friends had been,
  And all its famous places seen,
They travelled on, old Caen to see,
Another town in Normandy.

Arrived at Caen, the travellers here
Before the chief Hotel appear,
Miss Earle, Rose, Bertie you descry—
The rest are coming by-and-by.

Monsieur le Maitre, with scrape and bow,
Stands ready to receive them now,
And Madame with her blandest air,
And their alert *Commissionaire.*

NEXT up the staircase see them go,
  With *femme de chambre* the way to show.
Father and Dennis, standing there,
Are asking for the bill of fare.

Monsieur le Maitre, who rubs his hands
And says, "What are *Monsieur's* commands?"
With scrape and bow, again you see—
The most polite of men is he.

MENU

NOW that dinner is ordered, we 'll just take a peep
  At the cooks in the kitchen—just see! what a heap
Of plates are provided, and copper pans too ;—
They 'll soon make a dinner for me and for you.
French cookery 's famous for flavouring rare,
But of *garlic* I think they 've enough and to spare.

MENU

If we ask how their wonderful dishes are made,
I 'm afraid they won't tell us the tricks of the trade.
Do they make them, I wonder, of frogs and of snails ?
Or are these, after all, only travellers' tales
The names are all down on the " Menu," no doubt,
But the worst of it is that we can't make them out.

THE WASHERWOMEN OF CAEN

HERE the children
  Came next morn,
Walking by
  The river Orne;
Near the poplars
  On the green,
Where the Washerwives
  Are seen.
Here they looked
  At old Nannette,
Wringing out
  The garments wet;
Saw how Eugénie,
  Her daughter,
Soaked them first
  In running water;
Watched the washers
  Soaping, scrubbing,
With their mallets
  Rubbing, drubbing—
Working hard
  With all their might,
Till the clothes
  Were clean and white.

"L'HOMME qui passe," in France they call
  The man who thrives
  By grinding knives—
Who never stays at home at all,

  But always must be moving on.
    He's glad to find
    Some knives to grind,
  But when they're finished he'll be gone.

    With dog behind to turn the wheel,
      He grinds the knife
      For farmer's wife,
    And pauses now the edge to feel :

      The dog behind him hears the sound
        Of cheerful chat
        On this and that,
      And fears no knife is being ground.

        The man makes jokes with careless smile,
          He doesn't mind
          The dog behind,
        But goes on talking all the while.

THE

KNIFE-GRINDER

OF CAEN.

CHOCOLATE AND MILK.

LITTLE Lili, whose age isn't three years quite,
   Went one day with Mamma for a long country walk,
Keeping up, all the time, such a chatter and talk
Of the trees, and the flowers, and the cows, brown and white.
Soon she asked for some cake, and some chocolate too,
For this was her favourite lunch every day—
"Dear child," said Mamma, "let me see—I dare say

"If I ask that nice milkmaid, and say it's for you,
Some sweet milk we can get from her pretty white cow."
"I would rather have chocolate," Lili averred.
Then Mamma said, "Dear Lili, please don't be absurd:
My darling, you cannot have chocolate now:
You know we can't get it so far from the town.—
Come and stroke the white cow,—see, her coat's soft as silk."
"But, Mamma," Lili said, "if the *White* cow gives milk,
Then chocolate surely must come from the *Brown*."

LACE MAKERS OF CAEN

IN many a lowly cottage in France
The bobbins keep threading a mazy dance
The whole day long, from morning to night,
Weaving the lace so pretty and light.
How swiftly the nimble fingers twist
The threads on the pillow—not one is missed:
Each bobbin would seem to rise from its place
To meet the fingers that form the lace.
How wondrously quick the pattern shows
From the threads, as under our eyes it grows:—
How quickly follow stem, leaves, and flower,
As if under the spell of enchanter's power.
Look at old Nannette—she can scarcely see,
Yet none can make lovelier lace than she;
And her grand-daughter Julie—just seven years old,
Is learning already the bobbins to hold.
Without drawings to follow, or patterns to trace,
How can these poor cottagers fashion their lace?
From the plant and the flower and unfolding fern
And the frost on the pane their patterns they learn,—
From gossamer web by the spider wove,—
From natural taste and natural love
For every form of beauty and grace,
They 've learned to fashion their wonderful lace.

FOR Paris quite an early start
    They made the following day,
And out of windows every one
Kept looking, all the way.
And many a pretty road like this
The train went whizzing past,
Where gatekeeper, with flag and horn,
Stood by the gates shut fast.
That's Marie you see standing there :
Now, do you wonder why
A *woman* has to blow the horn
Before the train goes by ?—
Her husband is a lazy man,
He's in his cottage near,
He would not stir a step, although
The train will soon be here.
And Marie called him, " Paul, be quick—
Go shut the gate," she cried—
" Don't hurry me, there's time enough,"
The lazy man replied.
So Marie had to go, you see,
And take the horn, and blow.—
And every day it's just the same,
She always has to go.

· EN ROUTE ·

CLATTER ! clatter ! on they go,
Past stream and gentle valley,
Until the engine wheels turn slow,
And stop at length to dally

For dinner-time full half-an-hour
Within a crowded station,
While hungry little mouths devour
The tempting cold collation

Spread in the dining-room at hand ;
And then, when that is finished,
The children sally in a band,
With appetites diminished,

To look at all the folk they meet,—
The porters in blue blouses,
The white-robed priests, the nuns so neat,
The farmers and their spouses,

And all the other folk that make
A crowd in France amusing :—
Till hark ! their places all must take,
Without a minute losing.

The engine puffs—away they fly,
And soon leave all behind them;
Now turn the page, and you and I
In Paris safe will find them.

PARIS, gay Paris! so bright and so fair,
Your sun is all smiles, and there's mirth in your air.

The children, though tired with their travelling, found
That the first night in Paris one's sleep is not sound,
For the hum of the streets makes one dream all the night
Of the wonderful sights that will come with the light.

The morning was fine, and—breakfast despatched—
They soon made their way to the Gardens attached
To the old Royal Palace, and there met a throng
Of French children, and joined in their games before long.

One boy lent his hoop, and gave Bertie a bun,
And—talking quite fast—seemed to think it great fun
With nice English girls like our Nellie to play,
Though not understanding a word she might say.

On leaving the Gardens, the party were seated
Outside of a *café*, and there Papa treated
Them all to fine ices and chocolate too ;
They could hardly tell which was the nicer—could you?

Paris, gay Paris,
    So bright and so fair!
Your sun is all smiles.
    And there's mirth in your air!

IN THE TUILERIES GARDENS.

IN the Tuileries gardens, each afternoon,
  A little old man comes walking along :
Now watch what happens! for just as soon
As they see him, the birds begin their song,
And flutter about his hands and head,
And perch on his shoulder quite at their ease,
For he fills his pockets with crumbs of bread
To feed his friends who live in the trees,
And well they know he loves them so
That into his pockets they sometimes go.

But hark to what's going on over there!
'Tis surely a Punch-and-Judy man,
Making old Judy, I do declare,
Talk French as fast as ever she can!
And I think, from the looks of poor Mr. P.,
He's getting it hot from his scolding wife;
But just wait a minute, and then you'll see
He'll beat her within an inch of her life.
Walk in! take a seat and you'll see her beat,
And a penny is all you pay for the treat.

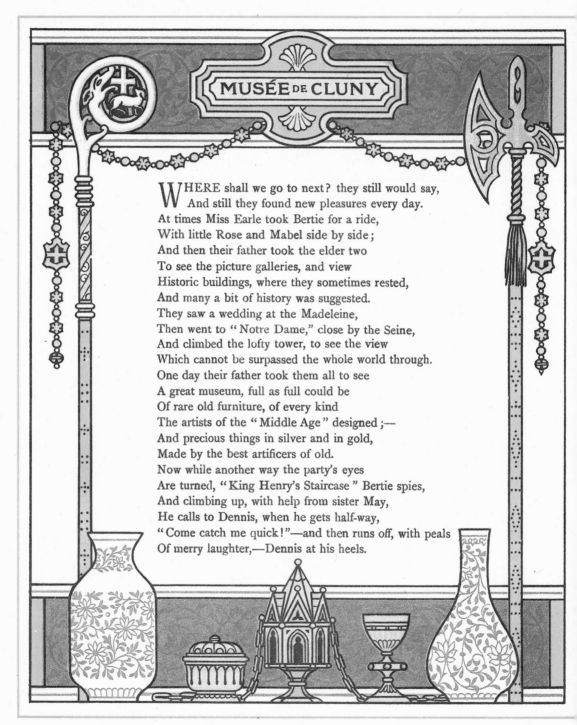

MUSÉE DE CLUNY

WHERE shall we go to next? they still would say,
    And still they found new pleasures every day.
At times Miss Earle took Bertie for a ride,
With little Rose and Mabel side by side;
And then their father took the elder two
To see the picture galleries, and view
Historic buildings, where they sometimes rested,
And many a bit of history was suggested.
They saw a wedding at the Madeleine,
Then went to "Notre Dame," close by the Seine,
And climbed the lofty tower, to see the view
Which cannot be surpassed the whole world through.
One day their father took them all to see
A great museum, full as full could be
Of rare old furniture, of every kind
The artists of the "Middle Age" designed;—
And precious things in silver and in gold,
Made by the best artificers of old.
Now while another way the party's eyes
Are turned, "King Henry's Staircase" Bertie spies,
And climbing up, with help from sister May,
He calls to Dennis, when he gets half-way,
"Come catch me quick!"—and then runs off, with peals
Of merry laughter,—Dennis at his heels.

BERTIE was first. "I've won the race," he cried;
  But soon upon his lips the triumph died,
And Bertie back in fear to Dennis ran:—
"Oh Dennis, look! I ran against that man!
He shook and rattled so, and wagged his head,
And gave me such a fright!" "Pooh!" Dennis said,
"He will not hurt!" And then he made a bow:—
Good-bye, old soldier, we must leave you now.

NEXT afternoon, while at the Zoo', a little tale they heard
  Of the elephant that's there, and you shall hear it word for word.

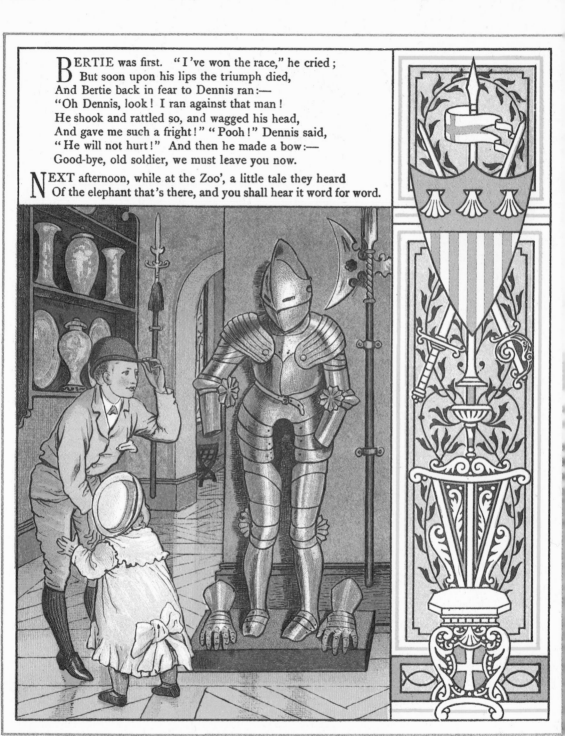

MUMBO and Jumbo, two elephants great,
    From India travelled, and lived in state,
In Paris the one, and in London the other :
Now Mumbo and Jumbo were sister and brother.
A warm invitation to Jumbo came,
To cross the Atlantic and spread his fame.
Said he, "I really don't want to go—
But then, they're so pressing!—I can't say No!"

So away to America Jumbo went,
But his sister Mumbo is quite content
To stay with the children of Paris, for she
Is as happy an elephant as could be :
"I've a capital house, quite large and airy,
Close by live the Ostrich and Dromedary,
And we see our young friends every day," said she ;
"Oh, where is the Zoo' that would better suit me?"

A STEADY steed is Mumbo, if just a trifle slow;
Upon her back you couldn't well a-steeple-chasing go :
But other opportunities there are to have a ride,
For there's a stud of ponies, and a camel to bestride—
A cart that's drawn by oxen can accommodate a few,

And if such queer conveyances don't please you at the Zoo',
There are little tramway cars too, with seats on either side,
Which will take you through the gardens, and through the *Bois* beside :—
Take the ticket on the other page, and with it you may go
From the lake within the garden to the gate that's called *Maillot*.

THE SWANS.

"Ho! pretty swans,
    Do you know, in our Zoo'
The swans of old England
    Are just like you?"

"Don't tell me!"
    Said a cross old bird;
"I know better,
    The thing's quite absurd.

"Their figures, I'm sure,
    Are not worth a glance:
If you want to see style,
    You *must* come to France."

With a scornful whisk
    The swan turned tail,
Spread its wings to the breeze,
    And was off full-sail.

"Ho! pretty swan,
    Do you know, in our Zoo'
The swans are not half
    So conceited as you?"

A FLOWER STALL ON

THE BOULEVARDS

LOOK at Mère Victorine
At her stall in the street.
With the lily and rose,
And the white *marguerite*,
She makes pretty *bouquêts*
The whole of the day:
There are buyers in plenty
Who pass by that way.
Little Basil and Amélie,
Watching her, stand:
Up to Mère Victorine
Basil stretches his hand,
"Can't you spare me," says he,
"A morsel of green,
Or *one* sweet little flower,
Good Mère Victorine?"
"If you come for a flower,
Pray where is your *sou?*"
Answers Mère Victorine,
"I can't *give* one to you—
Such flowers as mine
Are for selling, you know;
You must go to the country,
Where *wild* flowers grow."

A DAY AT VERSAILLES.

A T Versailles, as perhaps you have heard,
　　Countless pictures of fights
　　Form the chief of the sights:
Could so many great battles have ever occurred?

No wonder our children the gardens preferred :—
For the fountains were really so pretty a sight,
That Bertie declared—and I think he was right—
　　It was better to play
　　Like the fountains all day,
Than such terrible battles to fight.

LA
FONTAINE
DES INNOCENTS

ROUND this pretty fountain here
Sparrows gather all the year;
In its sparkling waters dip,
From its basin freely sip,
Round about their fountain play,
Safe and happy all the day;—
Little "innocents" are they.
That is Antoine, bread in hand;
See him by his mother stand:
Saucy little birdies spy
Antoine's bread, and at it fly,
Trying each to get a share,
Frightening little Antoine there.
Antoine does not *wish* to share,
Thinks the bread is all *his* right,
Just to suit his appetite.
Mother says, "Be kind, my son,
There is more when this is done;
Bread enough for thee at home:—
Let the pretty sparrows come;
Give them each a little crumb."

Here our little family
Near the fountain too, we see,
Walking through the open space
To the covered market-place.

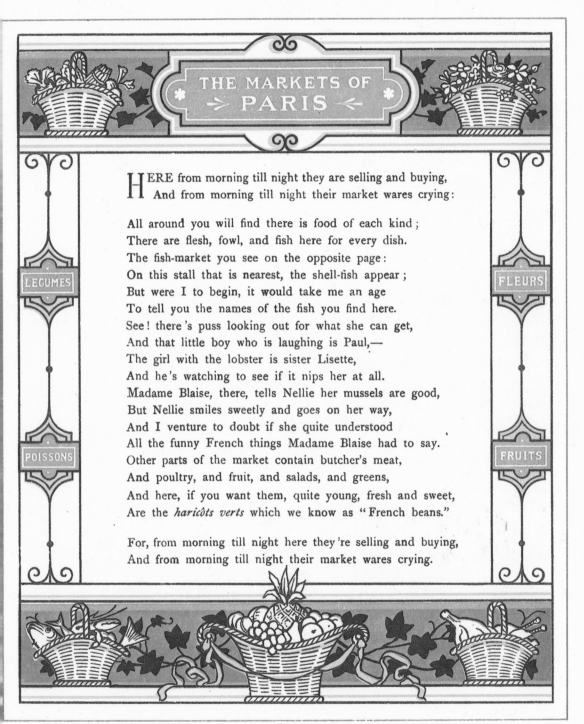

THE MARKETS OF PARIS

LEGUMES

POISSONS

FLEURS

FRUITS

HERE from morning till night they are selling and buying,
And from morning till night their market wares crying:

All around you will find there is food of each kind;
There are flesh, fowl, and fish here for every dish.
The fish-market you see on the opposite page:
On this stall that is nearest, the shell-fish appear;
But were I to begin, it would take me an age
To tell you the names of the fish you find here.
See! there's puss looking out for what she can get,
And that little boy who is laughing is Paul,—
The girl with the lobster is sister Lisette,
And he's watching to see if it nips her at all.
Madame Blaise, there, tells Nellie her mussels are good,
But Nellie smiles sweetly and goes on her way,
And I venture to doubt if she quite understood
All the funny French things Madame Blaise had to say.
Other parts of the market contain butcher's meat,
And poultry, and fruit, and salads, and greens,
And here, if you want them, quite young, fresh and sweet,
Are the *haricôts verts* which we know as "French beans."

For, from morning till night here they're selling and buying,
And from morning till night their market wares crying.

ROSE and Bertie have a ride ;
  Mabel, walking at their side,
Carries both the dolls, and so
By the Luxembourg they go.

Over in that Palace soon—
For the clock is marking noon—
The " Senate" will together come
(Like our " House of Lords" at home).

IN THE
LUXEMBOURG GARDENS.

Hear that woman, " Who will buy
Windmill, ball, or butterfly "—
Josephine and Phillipe, see,
Eager as they both can be.

Charles before her, silent stands,
With no money in his hands,
No more *sous*—he spent them all
On that big inflated ball.

Be content, my little friend,
Money spent you cannot spend ;
With your good St. Bernard play,
Buy more toys another day.

A
MERRY·GO
ROUND

HERE all the day long,
  Are race-horses for hire,
That never go wrong.
And besides, never tire.
Here all the day long,
Are race-horses for hire.

Who will come for a ride?
Horses, lions, all ready!
Bear or tiger astride,
You shall sit safe and steady.
Who will come for a ride?
Lions, horses, all ready!

Round and round they canter slow—soon they fast and faster go :
Look at Louis, all in white, Gaspard, almost out of sight,
Rose and Mabel side by side ;—Bertie watching while they ride.
Dennis waits till they have done,—much too big to join the fun ;
Brother Paul, with serious air, minds his little sister Claire,
Thinking if *he* had a sou, *she* should have some pleasure too.

IN THE
CHAMPS
ELYSEES

NOW, with regret, they've said Good-bye to Paris bright and gay;
To Calais they are drawing nigh—you see them on their way.
To travel thus, all through the night, at first they thought was fun.
But by degrees they grew less bright, as hours passed one by one.
Then Nellie to her sisters said, "Let's have an extra rug,
And make-believe we're home in bed, and cuddle close and snug,
And try, until the night has passed, which can most quiet keep."
Then all were tucked up warm and fast, and soon fell sound asleep.

CONTINENTAL BRADSHAW

The happy time abroad, again in dreams is all gone o'er—
Again in Paris, as it seems, they watch the crowd once more.
The "Elysian Fields," beneath the trees, are peopled with a throng
Of loveliest dolls, which at their ease converse, or ride along;
And wondrous "Easter Eggs" in nests, abundant lie around,
And "April Fish" with golden vests and silver coats, abound!
Such fleeting fancies Dreamland lends to pass the time away
Until the railway journey ends, just at the break of day.

PORTE DE LA MER, CALAIS.

THE last place where they stopped abroad was Calais, which, you know,
  Belonged to England once—though that was many a year ago:
It has a beautiful old Tower, all weatherworn and brown,
And here's the Sea-Gate, opening from the walls that guard the town.
But now Farewell to Merry France! the vessel ready waits
To take our party back again across the Dover Straits.

HOMEWARD BOUND.

HURRAH! we're afloat, and away speeds the boat as fast as its paddles can go,
  With the wind on its back, and a broad foaming track behind it, as white as the snow.
On board, every eye is strained to descry the white cliffs of our own native land,
And brightly they gleam, as onward we steam, till at length they are close at hand.
The sun shines with glee on the rippling sea, and the pennant strung high on the mast,
But at length it sinks down behind the grey town, and tells us the day is nigh past.
See, there is the port, and near it a fort, and the strong old Castle of Dover—
We're close to the shore—just five minutes more, and the Channel Crossing is over.
Then all safe and sound upon English ground, we bid farewell to the sea—
Jump into the train, and start off again as fast as the engine can flee.
We run up to town, and thence travel down to the home in the country, at night;
Then, I'm sorry to say, dear Nellie and May, Rose, Dennis, and Bertie bright,
We must leave in their home till next holidays come, when, let all of us hope, it may chance
That our trip will, next Spring, be as pleasant a thing as our swallow-flight over to France.

55

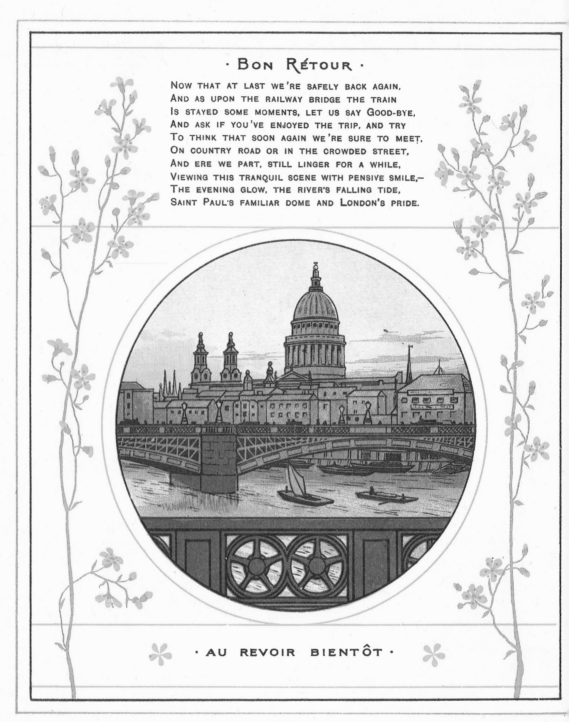

· Bon Rétour ·

Now that at last we're safely back again,
And as upon the railway bridge the train
Is stayed some moments, let us say Good-bye,
And ask if you've enjoyed the trip, and try
To think that soon again we're sure to meet,
On country road or in the crowded street,
And ere we part, still linger for a while,
Viewing this tranquil scene with pensive smile,—
The evening glow, the river's falling tide,
Saint Paul's familiar dome and London's pride.

· AU REVOIR BIENTÔT ·

56